In loving memory of Tootie and Bobby Pin
— R.T.H.

Copyright © 2008 by Ryan T. Higgins

Cocklebury Books
2nd Floor
4 Lyndon Way
Kittery, ME 03904

www.cockleburybooks.com

First Edition: 2008

ISBN-13: 978-0-9815007-0-6
ISBN-10: 0-9815007-0-6
Library of Congress Control number: 2008900557

10 9 8 7 6 5 4 3 2 1

Printed in Singapore
by Tien Wah Press

The illustrations for this book were drawn in pen and ink
and digitally colored in Adobe Photoshop. The text is set
in Papyrus and the title is set in Party LET. All other fonts
are either Garamond or Marker Felt. This book was made
on a Mac.

Twaddleton's Cheese

by Ryan T. Higgins

Cocklebury Books

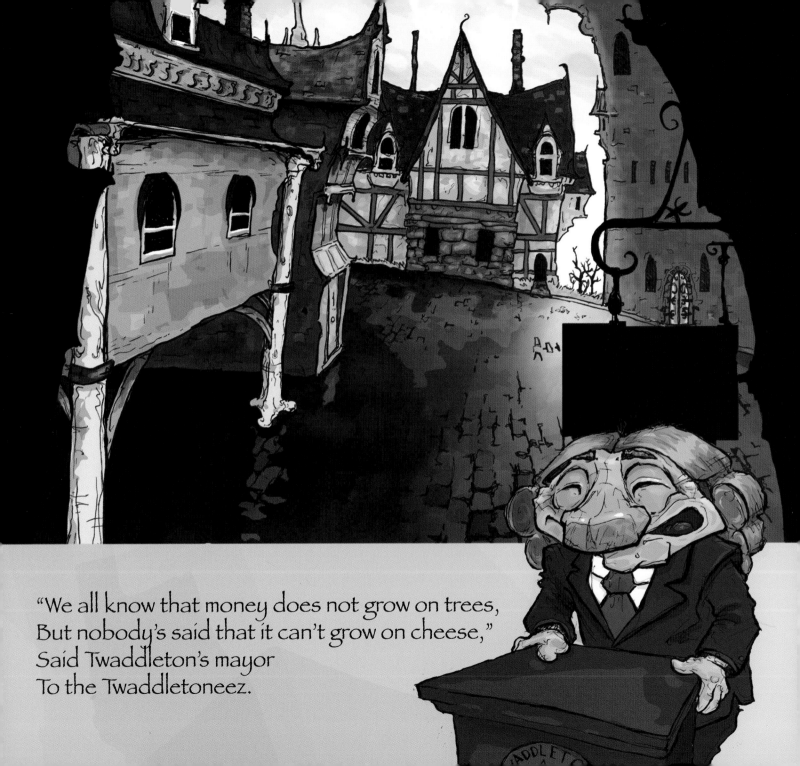

"We all know that money does not grow on trees,
But nobody's said that it can't grow on cheese,"
Said Twaddleton's mayor
To the Twaddletoneez.

He had a cheese factory built on a hill.
He hired cheese-makers with cheese-making skill.

But even before the first workday was through,
They made so much cheese no one knew what to do.

So they sold it as furniture...

'Til the whole town was full,
From the church to the jail.

But as the cheese gathered and grew rather old,
It didn't grow money. It only grew mold.

A town full of cheese isn't really that swell.
'Cause cheese in the breeze makes an unpleasant smell.

Something had to be done,
And done very quick...

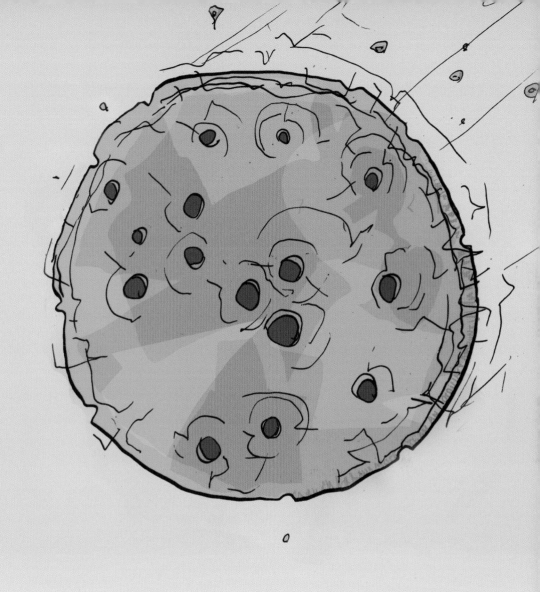

So they chucked off a cheese-wad one hundred feet thick.

At seven past two on the 12th of July
Four field mice were dashing, when out of the sky
There came a great object that fell like a brick,
A massive sized something one hundred feet thick.

But what was this thing that crashed down with a BOOM?
"Oh no!" cried the mice. "It's the moon! It's the moon!"

They wanted to help it. They needed a plan,
To put the "moon" back in its place.
The moon, it just doesn't belong on the land.
It belongs in the outers of space.

"The horizon's the place
Where the land meets the sky.
We should push the moon off it
And see if it flies."

They started off pulling, and tugging, and towing,
(With a "huff," and a "grunt," and a "wheeze")
What they thought was the moon. They had no way of knowing,
They were towing a great wad of cheese.

But soon they grew tired,
As little mice do,
'Cause a cheese-wad is bigger
To them than to you.

All hope was lost 'til they came to a sign,
Standing high and so proud did it say:

The four little mice went straight into town,
Looking for help, but all that they found
Were the screams and the shouts of the Twaddletoneez,
Who were mad at the mice for returning their cheese.

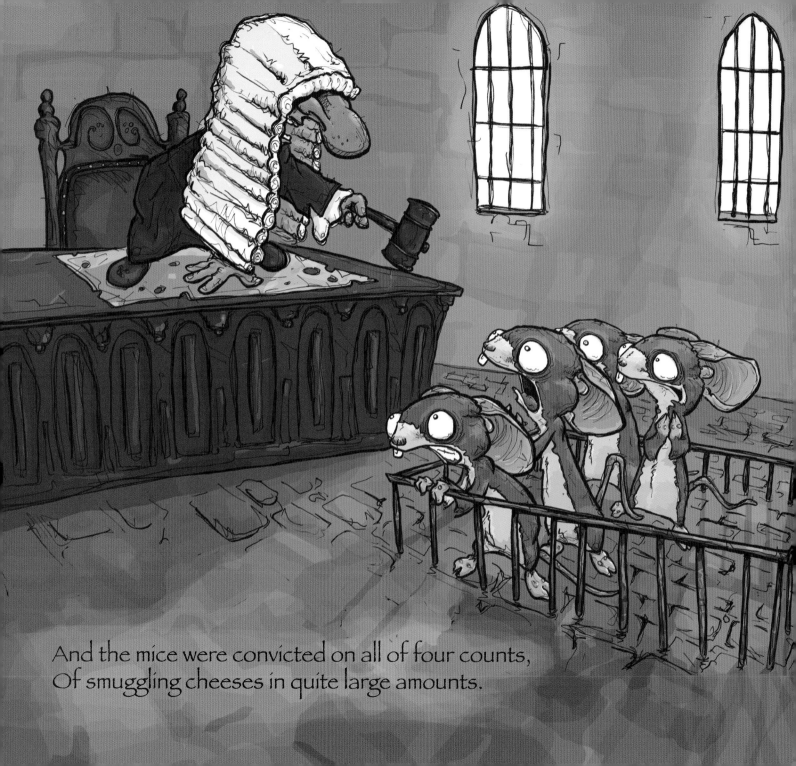

And the mice were convicted on all of four counts,
Of smuggling cheeses in quite large amounts.

"Please, Mister Judge. Please let us explain.
We're just little mice with rather small brains.
We promise we thought that your cheese was the moon.
We now know it's cheese and we'll solve this mess soon.
We'll eat it! We'll eat it! I and these three.
We'll eat it all up! We'll eat it. You'll see!"

Nobody thought they could actually do it.
But when the mice started, they really got to it.

And wouldn't you know it, they ate all the cheese.
"Huzza! Hurray!" cheered the Twaddletoneez.

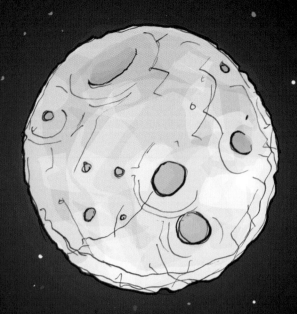

"In order to thank you, we'll donate one slice
Of our cheese, every day, to the hungriest mice.
All over the world, we will give it away."
And that's just what they did. (And still do to this day.)

The chubby mice waddled on back to their home,
Given cheeses in lifetime supply.
The sun started snoozing—too sleepy to roam—
And the moon found its way to the sky.

The End